KT-424-238

YOU AND YOUR CHILD
PAPERPLAY

Ray Gibson and Jenny Tyler

Illustrated by Sue Stitt, Simone Abel
and Graham Round

Designed by Carol Law

Edited by Robyn Gee

Photography by Lesley Howling

About this book

There is a great variety of things you can make using paper or card, scissors and glue, with a few extras. This book is designed to give you some ideas and starting points. Besides being fun, this type of activity can help young children to develop important skills such as hand control and coordination, concentration and decision-making, and broaden their understanding of concepts such as size, shape and measurement.

First published in 1990 by Usborne Publishing Ltd, Usborne House, 83-85 Saffron Hill, London EC1N 8RT, England. Copyright © 1990 Usborne Publishing Ltd. The name Usborne and the device ♔ are Trade Marks of Usborne Publishing Ltd. All rights reserved. No part of this publication may be reproduced, stored in any form or by any means, electronic, mechanical, photocopying, recording, or otherwise, without the prior permission of the publisher. Printed in Belgium.

Bee mobile

You will need: two colours of paper · pencil · ruler · round-ended scissors · paper glue · wool · white paper · felt-tip pen

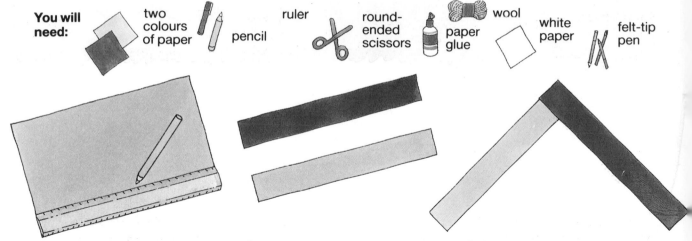

Line a ruler up along the edge of a piece of coloured paper. Draw a line.

Cut along the line. Make another strip using different coloured paper.

Stick the two strips together at one end, at right angles.

Repeat until all the paper is used up.

Stick the last piece down firmly.

Fold paper to cut two the same size.

Bend the bottom strip up and over the top strip. Press firmly.

Cut an upside down V shape into an end piece. Bend it down to make a nose.

Cut two wings and two eyes out of paper.

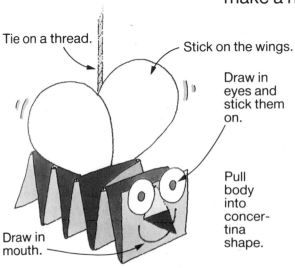

Tie on a thread.

Stick on the wings.

Draw in eyes and stick them on.

Pull body into concertina shape.

Draw in mouth.

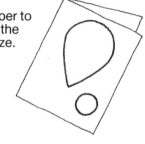

To make mobiles

Tie sticks of different ▶ lengths together. Plant support sticks are ideal.

Make several bees and hang them on threads from a coathanger. ▼

Snail mobile

You will need: paper, round-ended scissors, glue, black felt-tip pen, garden cane, wool, curtain ring

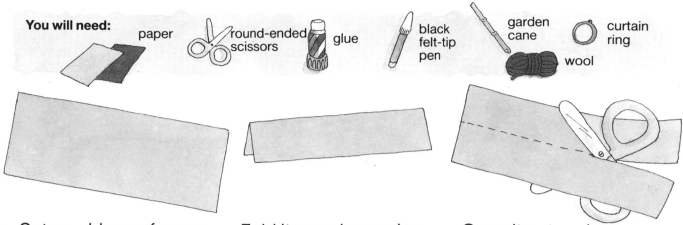

Cut an oblong of paper about 16cm by 3cm (6in by 1in).

Fold it over, long edge to long edge. Press to make a crease.

Open it out and cut along the crease to make two strips.

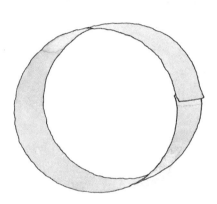

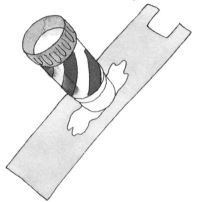

Put glue on one end of one strip. Stick the other end to it to make a circle.

Cut a small square out of the other strip to leave horns. Draw on eyes and a mouth.

Turn it over and put glue on the middle section.

Press firmly to make it stick.

Press the circle onto the glued section of the second strip. Lift up the head end.

Making a mobile

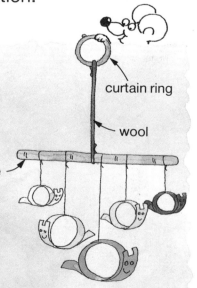

Make several snails and use wool to hang them from a stick as shown.

curtain ring

wool

garden cane

Balance the stick by sliding it left or right through the centre loop.

Funny faces

 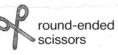

You will need: paper plates · magazines · round-ended scissors · glue · paper or wool

Cut out lots of eyes, noses, mouths and eyebrows from magazines.

Move them around a paper plate until you have the face you want, then stick them down. Add wool or paper hair if you like.

More simple collage ideas

Fridge food

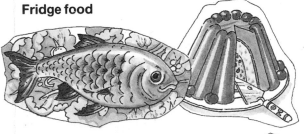

Discuss what kind of food you keep in the fridge and why. Stick some pictures of the food onto strong paper and cut round them. Fix onto the fridge to decorate it.

Car park
Draw out a car park. Discuss how you will arrange and stick down pictures of cars and lorries so they won't block each other in.

Tea table
Stick down paper doilies, or napkins for a tablecloth. Add pictures of cakes, cutlery, cups and plates.

Bendy snakes

You will need: magazines glue paper scissors felt-tip pens ruler

Use a ruler to help you cut straight lines.

Cut lots of coloured strips, some wide, some narrow, some long, some short, from a magazine.

Cut one end into a pointed tail, the other into a rounded head.

Draw and cut out lots of eyes. To get two eyes the same size, cut through two layers of paper.

Stick the eyes onto the heads of the snakes.

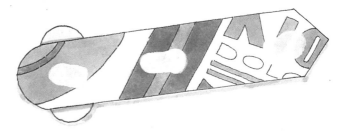

Turn the snakes over and put blobs of glue down their backs.

Stick them down in loops on paper.

Weave in and out of each other.

5

Trapeze artiste

You will need:
- wire coathanger
- straw
- pointed scissors
- round-ended scissors
- greaseproof paper
- sticky tape
- decorations (see opposite page)
- felt-tips
- paper-clips

To make the trapeze

Bend a wire coathanger to make a corner about 8cm (3in) from the hook.

Do the same on the other side.

Make some straight sides.

Straighten out the bottom bar.

Cut a piece of straw the same length as the bottom bar. Make a slit along it with pointed scissors*.

Press the straw onto the bottom bar. It should spin freely.

Lay some greaseproof paper on the template opposite. Secure it with paper-clips. Trace the figure with a thick crayon.

Colour the figure and draw in the face. Cut neatly round the outline, then stick on some decorations (see opposite).

Attach your person to the bar by curling her hands over and taping them in position.

Make her somersault over the bar, or hang the trapeze in a doorway, suspended from a piece of wool. Push it to make her fly through the air. Try putting her limbs in different positions.

6

*An adult should make the slit.

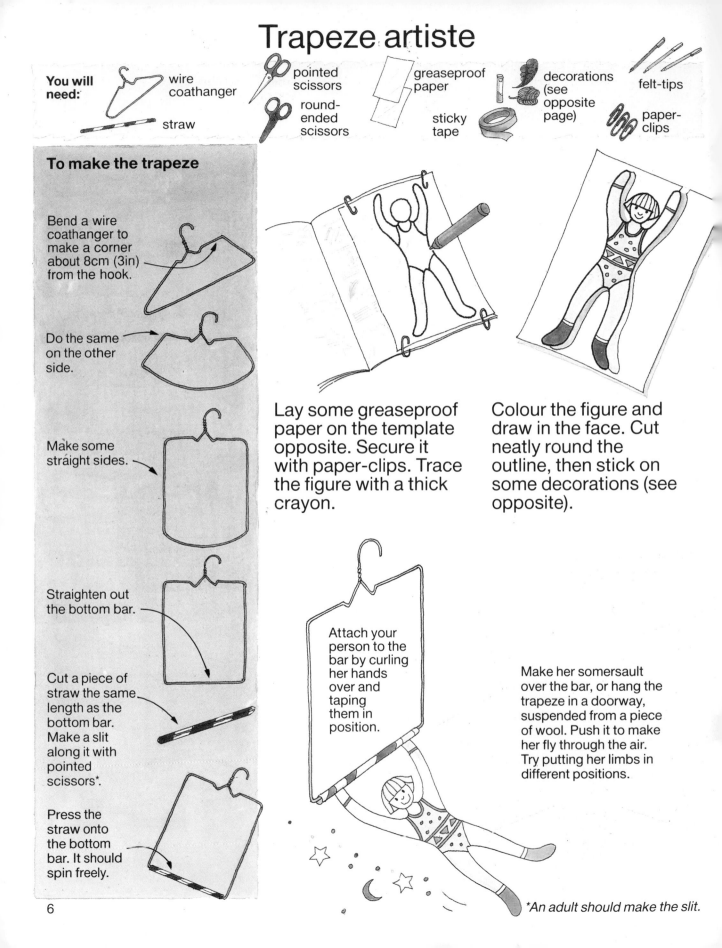

Some ideas for decorating the costume

◀ Felt-tip pens

Scraps of wool ▶

◀ Glitter

Sequins ▶

Feathers from a feather duster. ▼

Gummed paper shapes ▲

Ribbon ▶

Other ways to decorate your trapeze artiste

Give her wool hair. Only use a little, or the head will be too heavy.

Tie bows round her legs and arms. Use wool or silk thread.

Trace round the line and cut out.

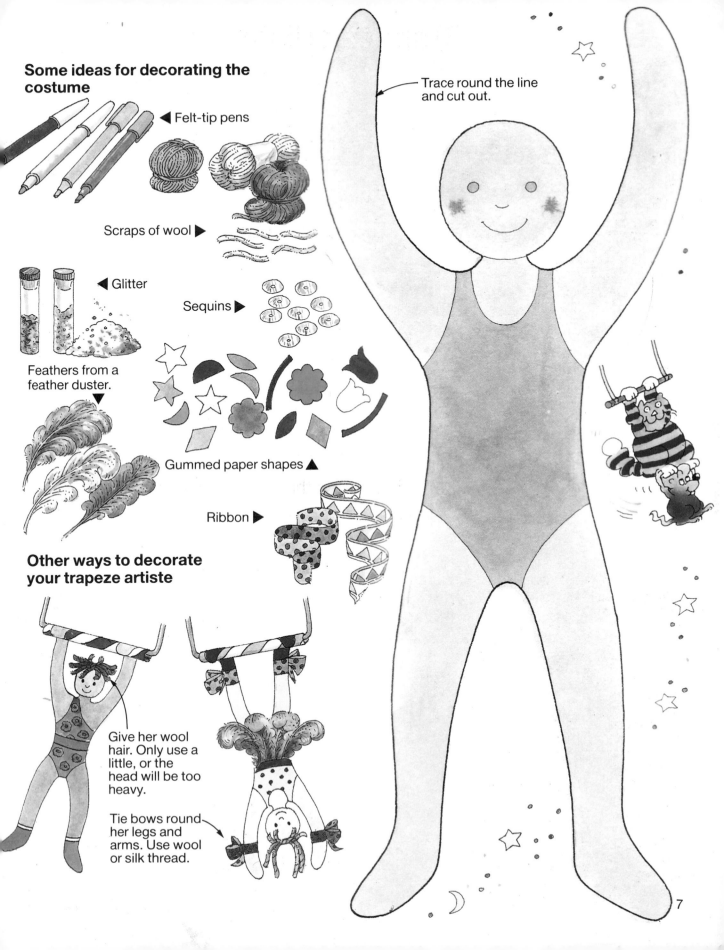

Owl and pussycat

You will need: 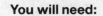  wallpaper  gluestick round-ended scissors 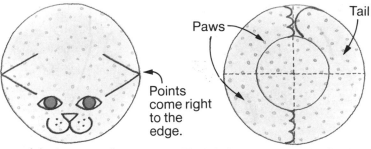 saucer

To make the pussycat

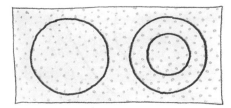

Make two circles on a piece of wallpaper by drawing round a saucer. Cut them out. Inside one, use a jar lid to draw a smaller circle.

Cut two V shapes for the ears in the plain circle. Draw a cat's face on the front half.

Points come right to the edge.

Paws   Tail

Fold the second circle into quarters, then open it out. Draw and cut out two paws and a tail.

Complete the head by bending up the ears. Glue the underside of point B and overlap onto point A each side.

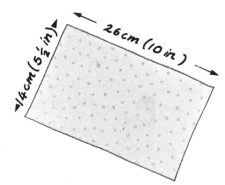

26cm (10in)

14cm (5½in)

Using more wallpaper, draw and cut out a rectangle, 14cm by 26cm (5½in by 10in)

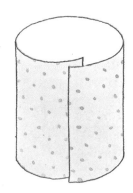

Bend the rectangle into a cylinder, overlapping it by about 2cm (1in). Stick the ends together.

Place the cat's head on its body.

Glue the top and inside edges of the paws before sticking.

Stick the tail on so that it can be seen from the front.

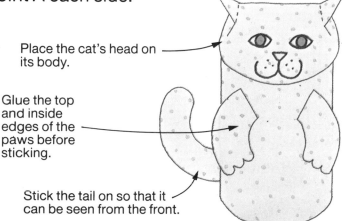

Hint

To make a nice even cylinder shape, wrap the paper strip round a can of food. Stick down the edges, then slide the tin out.

8

  jam-jar lids

  felt-tip pens

 ruler

thin,green paper

To make the owl

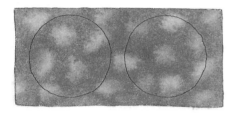

Make two circles on a piece of wallpaper by drawing round a saucer. Cut them out.

On one circle draw and cut out ears. Give your owl large round eyes and a beak.

Fold the other circle in half. Snip with scissors around the lower quarters, then cut down the fold line.

Complete the head as for the cat, but do not bend the ears up.

Cut a rectangle as for the cat. Bend the strip into a cylinder and stick down.

Overlap the wings and stick them together. Stick the wings to the cylinder.

Place the head onto the body.

Snip some toes at the front. Bend them upwards.

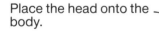

Other ideas to try

Make an owl or a cat family. Use jar lids for templates to make kittens and owlets. Make the bodies smaller too.

To make a tree for your owl make a bigger version of the sea anemone on page 11.

9

Magic boxes

You will need:

 shoe box with lid

sharp scissors for adults to use

 sticky tape

round-ended scissors

felt-tip pens

 paints and large brushes

thread

straws

Flying ghost box

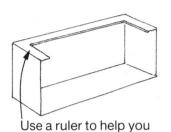

Use a ruler to help you draw the borders.

Turn a shoe box onto one long side. Cut out the top, using sharp scissors*, leaving a 2cm (1in) border on three sides.

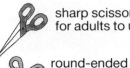

Pierce a hole in the lid with sharp scissors*. Cut out the centre, leaving a 2cm (1in) border all the way round.

Cut a hole in one side, so you can shine a torch into the box with the light off.

Stick lid on to front of box.

Paint the inside of the box.

Stick on torn strips of paper for trunks and branches.

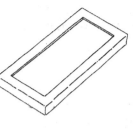

To make a ghost, pinch a piece of white toilet tissue in the centre, so that the corners hang down. Draw on black eyes. Hang from a thread fastened to a straw.

Add a bat to swoop around.

Draw some strange shapes for spooks. Colour them and cut them out. Hang them from straws.

Cut a trap door out of paper. Stick one side to the floor, so that it can move up and down.

Jumping-up skeleton

Draw a skeleton on white paper and then cut an outline round it.

Fold it as shown and attach a thread to the back of its head with sticky tape.

Glue the bottom onto the floor of the box. Pull the thread to make it jump up.

10

An adult should do the cutting.

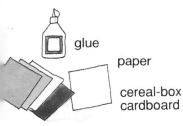
glue

paper

cereal-box cardboard

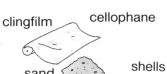
torch

white toilet tissue

clingfilm

cellophane

sand

shells

sponge

pebbles

Aquarium

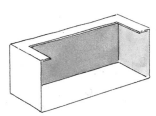

Cut out the side of the box and the lid as for the ghost box.

Paint blue water and a yellow, sandy floor inside the box.

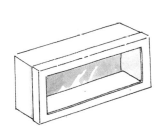

Use tape to stick clingfilm over the inside of the lid, so that it looks like glass.

Glue or tape the lid onto the front.

Stick torn coloured strips onto the sides to make seaweed or coral.

Draw fish on card or paper. Colour both sides and cut out. Attach thread and hang from straws.

Put shells, pebbles, bits of sponge and sand on the bottom. If you have no sand you can colour a little sugar with drops of food colouring.

Cut out and hang a cellophane jellyfish.

To make a sea-snake, see the bendy snakes on page 5.

To make an octopus, copy the spider on page 18.

Sea anemone

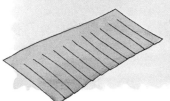

Cut slits in a strip of paper.

Roll the paper up and tape it at the bottom.

Gently pull the centre up.

Stand it upright by pressing it into a ball of dough or plasticine.

11

Super-glider

You will need: thin, strong paper · ruler · round-ended scissors · pencil · glue · large-headed drawing pin 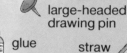 straw

 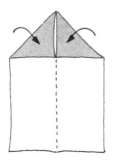  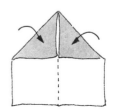

Measure and cut a rectangle 10cm by 15cm (4in by 6in). Make a crease down the centre by folding it in half. Open it out and turn it over.

Turn the top corners down, so that the points meet in the centre.

Turn the top triangle down.

Turn the top corners down, so the points meet in the centre.

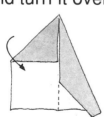 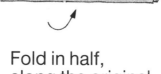 

Turn the two top sides of the triangle in, so the points meet in the centre.

Fold in half, along the original centre crease.

Turn upside down. Pull the wings up until they are level. Hold between your finger and thumb underneath and launch.

Windmill

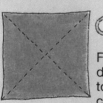

Cut a square of paper, 10cm by 10cm (4in by 4in).

Fold diagonally to make creases.

Cut from each corner along the creases, almost to the centre.

Glue and turn up every other point. Stick them together in the centre, overlapping slightly.

Press a large-headed pin through the centre of the windmill and into the top of a straw. Blow hard to make it whirl, or hold it in a strong wind.

Submarine

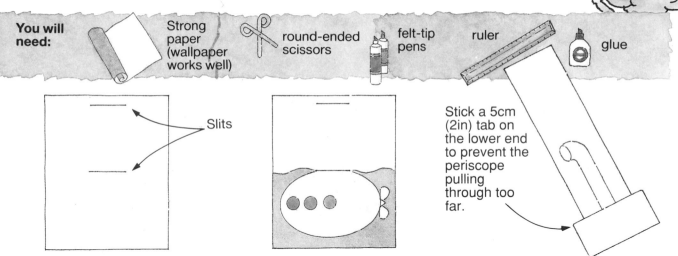

You will need: Strong paper (wallpaper works well) · round-ended scissors · felt-tip pens · ruler · glue

Slits

Cut a sheet of paper about 12cm by 15cm (5in by 6in). Make two 4cm (1½in) slits, as shown.

Draw the surface of the sea and a submarine, making its top level with the lower slit. Colour them in.

Stick a 5cm (2in) tab on the lower end to prevent the periscope pulling through too far.

Cut a strip 3cm (1½in) wide and 4cm (2in) longer than your paper. Draw a periscope on the lower half.

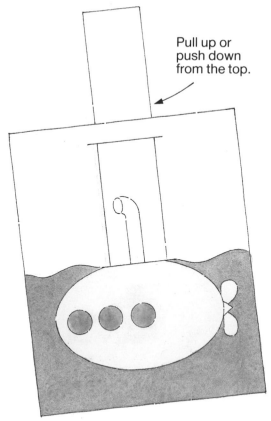

Pull up or push down from the top.

Thread the strip through the slits. Pull up from the top to raise the periscope.

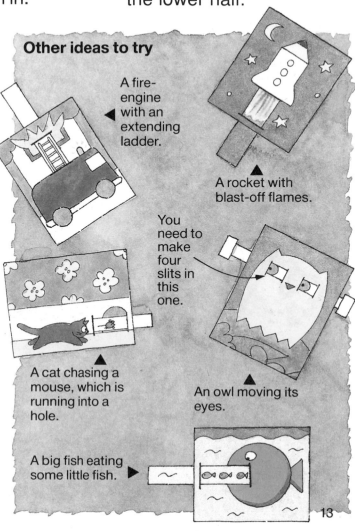

Other ideas to try

A fire-engine with an extending ladder.

A rocket with blast-off flames.

You need to make four slits in this one.

A cat chasing a mouse, which is running into a hole.

An owl moving its eyes.

A big fish eating some little fish.

13

Cars and roads

You will need: stiff paper   round-ended scissors   felt-tip pens or paints

Draw cars, lorries, motorbikes, bicycles, trees, shops etc. along the straight edges of your paper. Colour them in bright colours.

Put glue here.

Cut them out, keeping a straight edge at the bottom.

To make stands, cut strips of cereal box card about 2cm (¾in) wide and twice the height of the drawing.

Fold, as shown, and put glue on the end tabs.

glue

sticky tape

empty matchboxes

straws

cereal box

Use two stands for wide pictures.

To make road signs and bridges, see below.

Stick the stands to the back of the drawings. Make sure the lower glued flap is in line with the bottom edge of the paper.

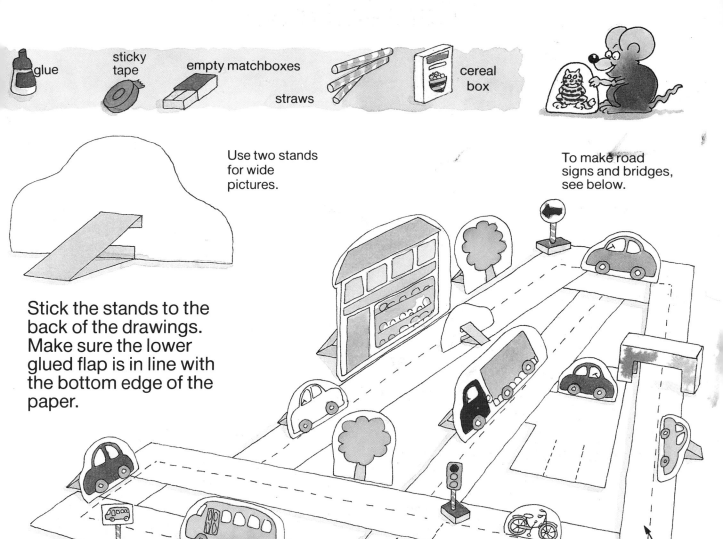

Draw in centre markings.

For roads join strips of paper together with sticky tape. Put some at right angles to make junctions and corners.

Other ideas to try

Road signs

Draw and cut out road signs.

Stick a cut-down straw to the back.

Make a hole in a matchbox with a pencil point. Push the straw into the hole.

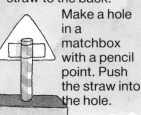

Bridge

Cut a cereal box in half. Cut a rectangle wider than the road from each side.

Animal zoo

Draw and cut out lots of different animals and fix them onto stands, as for the cars and buildings above.

15

Paper money and wallet

You will need: white paper, coloured paper, felt-tip pens or crayons, sticky tape, glue, soft pencil, coins, ruler

Cut out some pieces of paper the size and shape of money notes. On each one write a number to show how much it is worth and draw a picture.

For your wallet, cut a piece of coloured paper 2cm (¾in) wider than your paper money and one and a half times as high.

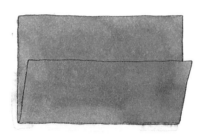

Fold up the bottom edge by about a third.

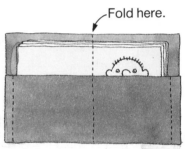

Fold here.

Stick down the sides to make a pocket. Put the money in it and fold it in half.

Rose

Write your name on the front and then decorate it.

Other ideas to try

Coins
Lay thin paper over real coins. Hold it firmly in place while you rub over them with a soft pencil. Stick card on the back and cut them out.

Stamps
Draw a small box. Draw or stick a small picture in the centre. Cut it out.

Envelopes
Fold a square of paper diagonally in both directions. Open it out. Centre

Fold the bottom corner up to the centre. Fold in each of the two side corners, overlapping the edges slightly.

Glue or tape down the edges. Fold the remaining top corner down to make the flap.

Racing rafts

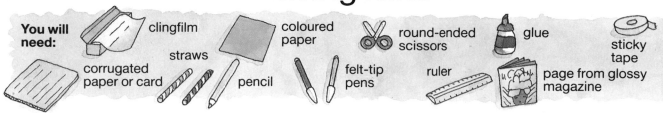

You will need: corrugated paper or card, clingfilm, straws, coloured paper, pencil, felt-tip pens, round-ended scissors, ruler, glue, sticky tape, page from glossy magazine

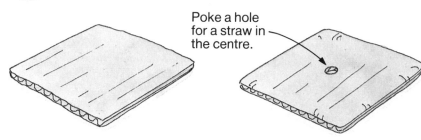

Poke a hole for a straw in the centre.

Cut a square of corrugated paper.

To make it last longer, wrap clingfilm around it and stick the edges down.

Cut out a square of coloured paper for a sail and decorate it. Poke a small hole in the centre top and bottom.

Try racing two or more rafts in the sink or bath. Blow hard into the sails.

Thread the sail onto a straw and push one end of the straw firmly into the raft. Cut the straw down if necessary.

Rowing boat

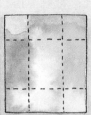
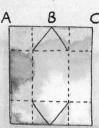

Cut a rectangle 9cm by 5cm (3½in by 6in) out of a glossy magazine. Mark the centre of each side.

Fold each side in turn to the centre. Crease and open out.

Make a cut from the centre of each short side to where the fold-lines cross.

◀ Bring points A and C together behind B. Glue them together where they overlap. Glue triangle B over them. Repeat at the other end.

Cut a strip of paper 7cm by 2cm (2¾ by ¾in). Fold down the ends 1cm (½in). Glue and stick onto the boat to make a seat.

Cut some straws and poke through the side for oars.

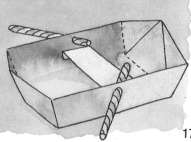

Paper puppets

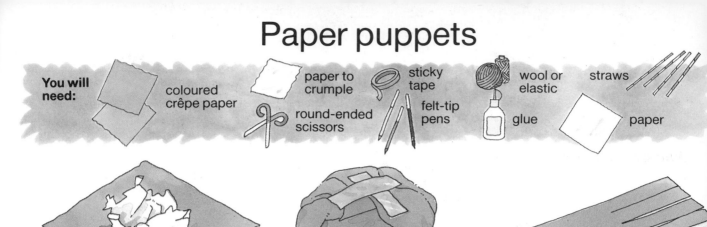

You will need: coloured crêpe paper, paper to crumple, round-ended scissors, sticky tape, felt-tip pens, wool or elastic, glue, straws, paper

Place a crumpled ball of paper on a large square of crêpe paper.

Gather up the crêpe paper and stick it down with tape to make a ball.

Cut an oblong of coloured paper. Snip long cuts down each short side.

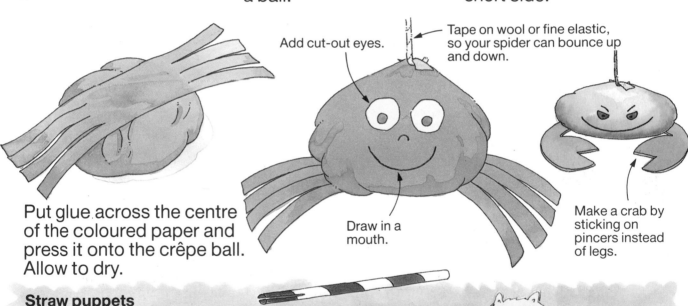

Put glue across the centre of the coloured paper and press it onto the crêpe ball. Allow to dry.

Add cut-out eyes.

Tape on wool or fine elastic, so your spider can bounce up and down.

Draw in a mouth.

Make a crab by sticking on pincers instead of legs.

Straw puppets

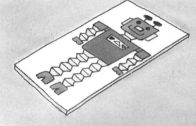

Draw and cut out some characters from a story you like.

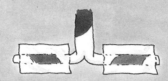

For each character cut a slit in one end of a straw.

Press the split ends onto the back of the puppet and stick down firmly to make a handle.

18

You will need:

thin cardboard and paper

round-ended scissors

felt-tip pens

cotton wool or wool

glue and sticky tape

paper bag

rubber bands

Dancing puppets

Round off the top with scissors.

Cut a piece of card 2cm (1in) wider than the width of two fingers.

Make two holes near the bottom to poke your fingers through.

Draw on faces.

Stick on cotton wool or wool hair.

Push just past second joint.

Push your fingers through the back and make your puppet dance around.

Paper-bag puppets

Draw a face on one side of an upside down paper bag.

Twist the corners for ears. Put your hand in the bag and fix round your wrist with a rubber band.

Finger-end puppets

Bend the strips round the ends of your fingers and stick to fit.

Add some hair.

Add some ears.

Cut strips of paper about 2cm (1in) wide by 5cm (2in) long.

Draw a face in the centre of each strip.

19

Costumes and disguises

You will need:

 paper plates 18cm (7in) diameter

 pencil

 round-ended scissors

felt-tip pen

 yoghurt carton

sticky tape or glue

wool

doily

Mr Wolf mask

Cut holes for your eyes and a space for your nose, in a paper plate.

Cut a section from a yoghurt pot, as shown.

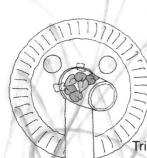

Tape or glue the yoghurt pot onto the plate, cut side downwards.

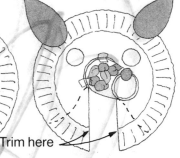

Trim here

Add ears and a nose cut from stiff paper. Trim away sharp edges, so you can speak easily.

 Cut along lines.

Fold some paper as shown and cut along lines to make teeth.

Poke holes at sides of plate and fix wool or elastic through.

Paint the mask if you like.

Stick teeth around cut section of yoghurt pot.

Other masks to try

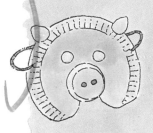

The three little pigs
Cut a yoghurt pot down to make a snout. Stick on as for the wolf. Draw in nostrils and paint. Add ears. Trim the sharp edges.

Goldilocks and the three bears
Cut the centre out of a doily to make a lace collar for Goldilocks.

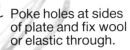

Make the bears' ears round. Stick on noses. Trim sharp edges.

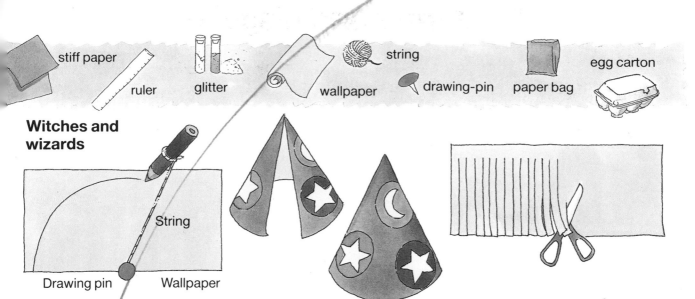

stiff paper

ruler

glitter

wallpaper

string

drawing-pin

paper bag

egg carton

Witches and wizards

String

Drawing pin · Wallpaper

For a hat draw a semicircle by tying string to a pencil and drawing an arc. Cut along the line.

Stick the edges together to fit your head size. Paint and decorate.

For hair, snip a band of paper and stick inside the hat.

To make a star draw two overlapping triangles, then cut round their outer lines. Spread glue on the star and sprinkle glitter over it. Shake off the excess glitter, then stick on the end of a plastic ruler.

Cut long nails from folded paper and tape onto finger ends.

Other fancy dress ideas

Posh woman
Make a tiara by folding a doily in half. Stick on crumpled sweetpapers or tinfoil for jewels. Use hairclips to fasten onto head.

Posh man
Draw a big bow-tie, colour it and cut it out. Pin it onto clothes.

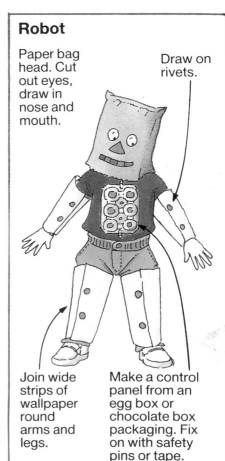

Robot

Paper bag head. Cut out eyes, draw in nose and mouth.

Draw on rivets.

Join wide strips of wallpaper round arms and legs.

Make a control panel from an egg box or chocolate box packaging. Fix on with safety pins or tape.

Surprise doors

You will need: two large sheets of wallpaper · non-fungicidal wallpaper paste · large paste-brush · round-ended scissors · felt-tip pens or paints

On a big piece of paper draw a large castle or house, with plenty of doors and windows.

Cut round the doors and windows, so they will open and shut.

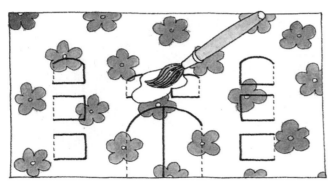

Cover the back of the picture, except the doors and windows, with paste. Stick it down onto the white side of another piece of wallpaper. Leave it to dry.

Open up the doors and windows so you can draw what's going on inside. Make up a story about it.

Other ideas to try

Kitchen
Make a kitchen with fridge, cupboards, washing machine and freezer.

Show what is inside each of them.

Ship
Make a ship with big portholes that will open and shut.

Show what the sailors, passengers and captain are all doing.

22

Family portrait book

You will need: wallpaper or sugar paper • glue • round-ended scissors • felt-tip pens • white drawing paper

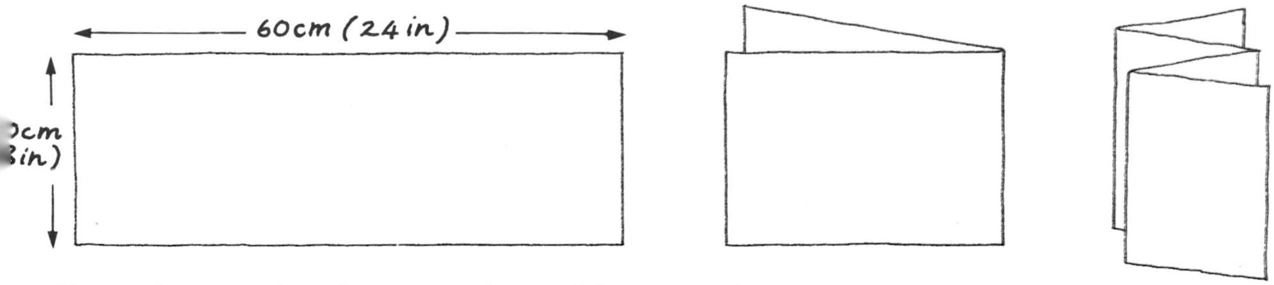

←—— 60cm (24in) ——→

20cm (8in)

Cut a long strip of paper about 60cm (24in) long and 20cm (8in) wide.

Fold it in half and then fold again as shown above.

dad   sister   gran is nice   ginger cat

You can use the other side as well.

Stick here.

Cover

For the cover cut another strip, twice as long as the folded up strip, plus 5cm (2in). Stick the first folded section inside the cover.

Draw some pictures of your family and stick them into the book. Write some captions underneath.

Other ideas to try

Alphabet book
Use a scrapbook, or fold sheets of paper together to make a book. Draw a big letter on each page, then draw or cut out and stick in things beginning with that letter.

Holiday book
Make a folding book, as above, showing what you did on holiday.

Story book
Make a folding book to tell a simple story.

Write about the people in the pictures.

The lost dog   A man finds the dog   address is on the collar   and he takes her home

23

Jewellery

You will need: wrapping paper or other colourful paper paper glue wool or fine elastic large blunt needle 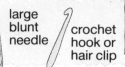 crochet hook or hair clip felt-tip pens straw pencil

Straw beads

Cut strips of patterned paper the length of a straw and about 8cm (3in) wide. Cover them with glue on the plain side.

Lay a straw on one long edge and roll the paper round it as firmly as you can. Leave to dry. Repeat this process several times.

Cut the straw beads into any length you like. If the ends flatten squeeze them into round shapes again.

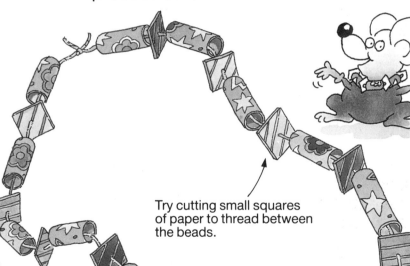

Try cutting small squares of paper to thread between the beads.

If you have no wrapping paper, colour some white paper yourself, or use pages from an old magazine or catalogue.

Brooches

Draw or cut out pictures you like to stick onto cereal-box card.

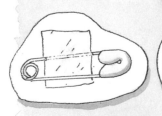

Attach a safety pin at the back with tape to make a brooch.

Thread with fine wool or elastic using a needle or crochet hook to pull the wool through. When it is long enough to slip over your head, tie in a knot.

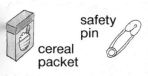 cereal packet

 safety pin

 sticky tape

 small jar lid

round-ended scissors

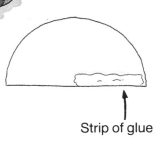

Matching earrings

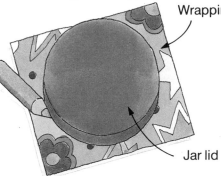

Wrapping paper

Jar lid

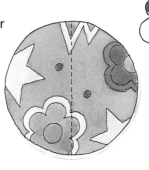

Strip of glue

Draw round a small jar lid to make a circle. Cut the circle out.

Fold the circle in half, then cut along the fold line.

Put a strip of glue halfway along each straight edge on the wrong side.

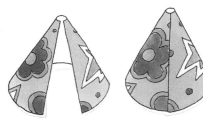

Bend round and overlap the edges to make a cone. Stick down firmly. Snip the top off the cone.

Loop some wool through the cone using a crochet hook or hair clip to help you thread it through.

Stick the ends inside the cone, leaving the loops to hang over your ears.

Ideas for bracelets

Cut two strips of different-coloured paper, one to fit round your wrist and one much longer.

Wrap the long piece round the short piece to give a striped effect. Join the ends with sticky tape to make a circle. Glue down the ends and trim.

Make a long concertina shape, by folding two bits of paper across each other at right angles. Stick into a circle.

Make a bracelet using straw beads threaded onto string or elastic.

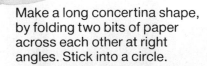

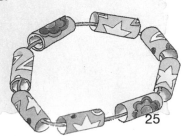

25

Greetings cards

You will need: white paper  stiff, coloured paper felt-tip pens or crayons  round-ended scissors

Pop-up cards

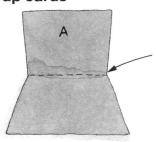

Press firmly along the folds to make a crease.

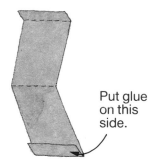

Put glue on this side.

Cut an oblong piece of paper (A) and fold the longest sides in half.

Cut a strip (B) about 3cm (1in) wide and half the length of A. Fold in half.

Open it out, turn it over, fold each end up about 1cm (½in). Glue each end.

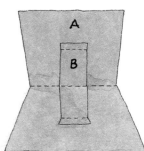

Lift the top half of A towards you so that B stands out.

When you open the card the picture will pop up.

Lay B down the centre of A, glue side down, so that the creases exactly correspond.

Colour and cut out a picture to cover the lower half of B. Stick it on.

Write your message here.

Name cards

Make an oblong card long enough to write your chosen name in big letters. Write the name onto it.

Stick little pieces of screwed-up sweet wrappers or tissue over the letters you have drawn. You can also make them into patterns.

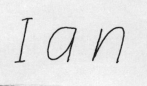

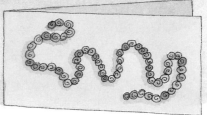

glue

 tissue paper or sweetpapers

 old photos

 paper fasteners
ruler

Contrast cards

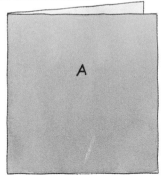

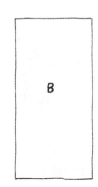

Fold an oblong piece of paper in half to make a card (A).

Cut another piece (B), half the width of the front, in a different colour.

Cut deep shapes from the right-hand side of (B). Save all the pieces you have cut.

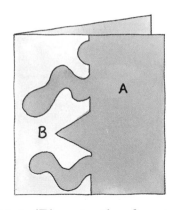

Stick (B) onto the front left half of (A).

Turn over the cut-out pieces and stick them down opposite the corresponding shapes, so that they mirror each other.

Other ideas for cards

Paper fastener cards
Use paper fasteners to fix separate parts, such as ears or wheels onto your cards. Poke the holes first with a pencil.

Photo cards
Cut some faces of your family from unwanted photos. They can be quite small.

Stick them onto a card, then draw a picture round them.

Paper presents

You will need:  paper  felt-tip pens 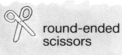 round-ended scissors  old magazines glue

Hand bookmark

Draw round your hand with a felt-tip pen.

Colour the hand brightly.

Cut it out carefully.

Stick onto a strip of paper and use it to put in a book so that the fingers show your place.

Willy worm bookmark

Draw, colour and cut out a worm. He should be longer than the height of a book so that his head and tail will stick out.

Give your worm some clothes, or draw on things like glasses or a bowtie.

28

 cereal box

 clingfilm

sticky tape

 wallpaper paste (non-fungicidal)

 wallpaper brush

yoghurt pot

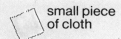 small piece of cloth

Mosaic place mat

Cut a large rectangle from a cereal box. Round off the corners with scissors.

Use a felt-tip pen to draw a big, bold design.

Find the colours you want to use in magazines. Tear them into pieces about 2cm (1in) square. Keep the colours separate.

Cover your dry mat with clingfilm taped on at the back.

Stick the coloured pieces onto the design.

Other ideas to try

Needle case
Fold a piece of stiff paper double to make a card. Draw a butterfly on it making sure the wings go right to the edge of the paper. Colour or decorate brightly and cut out double, so that it opens out.

Glue a small piece of cloth at the top only and stick onto the right side, for keeping needles in.

Write or copy your message on the left.

Pencil holder
Cover a yoghurt pot or cut-down plastic bottle with paper from an old comic or toy catalogue.

Hints

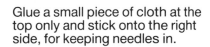

It is easier to paste the mat than the small bits of paper.

The more shades of each colour you use, the better the result.

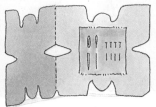

Paper bowls

You will need: cardboard egg carton cereal bowl and plate* 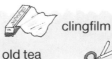 clingfilm electric food mixer old tea towel round-ended scissors sieve large bowl

Tear the egg box into pieces and soak in warm water in a large bowl until soft (10-20 mins.).

If you haven't got a mixer, squash the pieces up with your hands.

Tip some of the water into the food mixer. Switch it on and add the pieces gradually until you have a watery, mushy pulp.

Tip the mixture into a fine-mesh sieve over the sink. Press down to squeeze out most of the water.

Cover the bowl completely.

Place the upturned cereal bowl onto a plate. Cover it with clingfilm. Press small lumps of paper pulp all over it.

Place the tea towel over the bowl and press firmly all over, to flatten the pulp and remove excess water.

Use oven gloves to take it out.

Leave to dry in a warm place, or put in a microwave oven* and cook on a high setting for 10-12 mins., or until it is dry.

When the pulp has dried, remove it from the cereal bowl and trim round the edge with some scissors.

Paint and decorate your bowl with poster paints.

Other ideas to try

Try using egg boxes of two or more different colours in your bowls.

To make a stronger bowl, try kneading a little non-fungicidal wallpaper paste into the pulp after sieving.

*When using a microwave use only bowls and plates recommended for microwave use.

Materials and skills

The main equipment you will need to make the things shown in this book are paper, scissors, glue and felt-tip pens or paints. This page gives you advice on what type of glue, paper and scissors to use. The following page provides some tips and hints on cutting, folding and measuring.

The specific things you will need for each project are listed at the top of each page.

Scissors

All-plastic scissors can be fragile and not so good for use on stiffer papers or thin card. All-metal scissors can be heavy and awkward for children to use.

A good compromise is a pair of plastic scissors with a metal blade. These are often brightly-coloured and made in the shape of a bird, animal or fish.

Scissors should always be round-ended for safety and any adult's scissors should be put away out of reach immediately after use.

Glue

●Glue sticks are clean to use, with the gum easily directed to where you want it to go. Be sure to put the cap back after use. They can dry out quickly.

●Liquid glues and gums are useful and spread easily, but take longer to dry.

●P.V.A. (polyvinyl acetate) is good for sticking large areas. It is white but dries transparent. Protect clothing with aprons. Roll up sleeves. Wash brushes out carefully after use.

●Wallpaper paste is also good for large areas. It is very cheap and you can make up small batches as you need it. For safety always use the non-fungicidal type. If you have some left over, cover it with clingfilm and store in the fridge for use another day.

●Flour-and-water paste can be made up by making up a smooth paste, bringing to the boil and simmering for a few minutes. Make sure it is quite cool before use.

●Sticky tape is invaluable but can be tricky. Cut several strips and attach lightly at one end only to a suitable work-top edge ready for use.

Do not use solvent-based glues or instant bond glue.

Paper

White paper – use sheets from a writing pad, typing paper, drawer or wall lining paper, or other similar paper.

Stiff paper – use wallpaper or the covers of magazines.

Strong paper – wallpaper is fairly strong.

Thin, strong paper – typing paper, or something similar.

Dark or coloured paper – sugar paper, paper from magazines or wrapping paper.

Card – use cut-up cereal boxes or something similar.

Collecting a supply of paper

You can collect most of the paper you need for these projects, without having to buy anything specially.

It is a good idea to keep a drawer or box in which to store all the odd bits you manage to find.

Below is a list of things it is worth saving.

●coloured foil or cellophane sweet wrappers

●clear cellophane from flowers and boxes of pasta

●tissue paper from fruit or packaging

●thin cardboard - use cut-up cereal boxes or something similar.

●brightly-coloured pages from glossy magazines, leaflets or comics

●out-of-date catalogues

●corrugated paper is often used to pack china

●wrapping paper from birthdays or Christmas

●wallpaper is invaluable for its pattern value and strength and for its possibilities as drawing or painting paper

Materials and skills

Other good things to have

doilies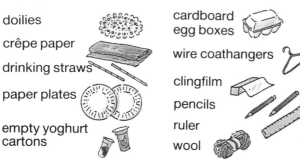

crêpe paper

drinking straws

paper plates

empty yoghurt
cartons

cardboard
egg boxes

wire coathangers

clingfilm

pencils

ruler

wool

Folding paper

Folding is often repetitive, so you could do one fold
and let your child copy you.

Point out before each step which edge is to be
lined up with which. Show your child how to hold
them firmly down while pressing in the crease.

Encourage her to check each time that the result
looks like the drawing.

Measuring

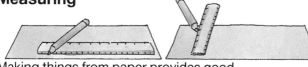

Making things from paper provides good
opportunities for learning about measuring.

You will probably need to do any accurate
measuring required yourself, but your child can
learn a lot from watching you, especially if you
explain carefully what you are doing.

When she is ready to try measuring for herself,
show her how to line the ruler up accurately and
mark off the required length with a pencil.

Using scissors

This may take a little time for a child to master. To
begin with she could be encouraged to cut along
straight lines. Let her draw some herself on
newspaper, using a ruler. She could then progress
to curved lines. Draw round a dinner plate to start
with, then progress to a tea plate, where the curve
will be sharper and so on.

On larger projects take it in turns to do the
cutting. As she becomes ready for them, show your
child the techniques explained in the next column.

Cutting round a shape

●Always cut a rough outline first,
this takes away an unmanageable
mass of paper.

●Encourage your child to hold the
paper lightly with her free hand
near to where she will cut, to avoid
tearing.

●Explain that she should not pull
on the paper, the scissors should
do the work.

●Demonstrate how to line up the
blades of the scissors along the
line to be cut to make it as accurate
as possible.

Cutting out a shape

●Poke a hole in the centre of the
shape to be removed with the
pointed end of a pencil.

●Insert the lower blade of the
scissors into the hole and cut to the
edge of the shape.

●Cut round it carefully and remove
it.

●If the paper is too stiff cut a slit in
the paper by bending, rather than
creasing the paper in the centre of
the unwanted area. Make a cut into
the folded edge, open out and
insert the scissors. Cut to the edge.